꽃

아시아에서는 《바이링궐 에디션 한국 대표 소설》을 기획하여 한국의 우수한 문학을 주제별로 엄선해 국내외 독자들에게 소개합니다. 이 기획은 국내외 우수한 번역가들이 참여하여 원작의 품격을 최대한 살렸습니다. 문학을 통해 아시아의 정체성과 가치를 살피는 데 주력해 온 아시아는 한국인의 삶을 넓고 깊게 이해하는 데 이 기획이 기여하기를 기대합니다.

Asia Publishers presents some of the very best modern Korean literature to readers worldwide through its new Korean literature series 〈Bilingual Edition Modern Korean Literature〉. We are proud and happy to offer it in the most authoritative translation by renowned translators of Korean literature. We hope that this series helps to build solid bridges between citizens of the world and Koreans through a rich in-depth understanding of Korea.

바이링궐 에디션 한국 대표 소설 069

Bi-lingual Edition Modern Korean Literature 069

Flowers

부희령

꽃

Pu Hee-ryoung

ASIA
PUBLISHERS

Contents

꽃

Flowers

여자가 보고 있는 것은 벽지에 그려진 꽃이다.

벽에 붙은 종이에 그려져 있는 그 꽃들은, 땅 속에 뿌리를 박고 피어난 자운영이나 능소화 같은 꽃들과 그 자태가 사뭇 다르다. 어물쩍 꽃이라는 이름으로 불리기는 했지만, 지금 여자의 눈앞에 있는 것은 채도가 낮은 분홍색과 보라색을 무딘 붓끝으로 뭉개놓은 얼룩에 지나지 않는다. 얼룩들은 옅은 비취색 배경 위에 일정한 간격으로 흩어져 있다. 세월의 때가 묻은 탓인지, 흰색이 많이 섞인 비취색 벽은 조금 의기소침해 보이기도 한다. 어쩔 수 없이 고집을 부리며 서 있는 듯한 '벽'이라는 사물에, 그 흐리멍덩한 의기소침함은, 의외로 잘 어

It's the flowers on the wallpaper that the woman is looking at.

The flowers on the paper pasted to the wall are totally different from real flowers, like Chinese milk vetches or trumpet creepers blooming with their roots embedded deep in the soil. Although vaguely referred to as "flowers," what the woman now sees are mere blotches of low-saturated pink and violet mashed together with the tip of a thick brush. The blotches are scattered at regular intervals and set against a weak jade-green background. The jade-green wall, which has a great deal of white mixed into it, looks rather melancholy—probably because

울린다고 여자는 생각한다.

여자는 얼마 전에 텔레비전에서 본 외국 드라마의 한 장면을 떠올린다. 십대의 여자애 둘이 전날 밤의 데이트에 대한 이야기를 나누고 있었다. 한 여자애가 묻는다. “그래서 너는 그 애에게 네 꽃을 바쳤니?” 질문을 받은 여자애가 짜증을 내며 대답한다. “꽃을 바치다니? 그게 무슨 말이야? 우린 그냥 섹스를 한 거라고!” 질문을 한 여자애는 뚱뚱하다. 그냥 뚱뚱한 게 아니라, 남자애와 데이트를 해본 적이 한 번도 없으리라는 생각이 들 정도로 비대한 몸이다. 첫 섹스의 경험을 이야기하던 여자애는 나긋한 허리를 돌려 뚱뚱한 여자애를 흘끔 바라본다. 그리고 그 자리를 떠난다. 섹스라는 말을 꽃이라는 단어로 얼버무리고 싶어 하던 여자애는 상기된 얼굴로 혼자 남았다……. 여자는 그 애의 얼굴이 눈앞에 보이는 벽지 속의 꽃들과 어딘지 닮은 데가 있다고 생각한다.

여성의 성기를 왜 꽃에 비유하는 것일까? 남성의 성기를 꽃으로 표현하는 것을 보거나 들은 적이 있었나? 여자는 새삼 기억을 더듬어본다. ‘나는 그의 꽃을 애무했다’ 또는 ‘그의 꽃이 몸 안으로 들어오는 것을 느꼈다’

it has accumulated so much dirt over the years. The woman thinks that this object, this "wall," appearing to stand so defiantly, goes unexpectedly well with the dull melancholy of the flower scene.

The woman recalls a scene from a foreign TV show she saw the other day. One girl asked, "So you offered your flower to the boy?" The other girl, irritated, answered, "Offered the boy a flower? What are you talking about? We just had sex." The girl who'd asked the question was overweight. She wasn't just overweight; she was so big as to make one think she'd never been out with a boy before. The girl talking about her first sexual experience turned her slim hips to give the overweight girl a sidelong glance, then she left. The overweight girl, who had wanted to talk about sex ambiguously by calling it a flower, was left alone, blushing. The woman thinks that the overweight girl's face somewhat resembles the flowers that she can now see on the wallpaper.

Why did people compare the female genitalia to a flower? Had anyone ever seen or heard someone compare the male genitalia to a flower? The woman quickly searches through her memory. Saying something like "I sucked his flower" or "I felt his

는 말은 어색하고 낯설다. 여성의 성기를 꽃에 비유하는 것은 오목한 생김새 때문일까? 여성의 성기는 꽃처럼 보고 즐길 수 있다는 의미일까?

여자는 언젠가 조지아 오키프라는 화가의 꽃 그림들을 본 적이 있다. 그림 속의 꽃들은 흘러내릴 듯 난만했고, 손가락으로 건드리면 물기를 뚝 떨어뜨릴 듯 보였으며, 나른한 어둠을 향해 무심하게 열려 있었다. 종이 위에 인쇄되어 있는 그림이라고 믿어지지 않을 정도로, 그것은 스스로 활짝 피어난, 진짜 꽃이었다.

여자는 한숨을 쉰다.

무료했던 사춘기의 어느 날, 여자는 자신의 성기를 들여다본 적이 있다. 손거울을 들이대고 한껏 다리를 벌린 다음, 고개를 숙여 들여다보았던 그것은, 꽃처럼 보였던가? 아니, 그렇지 않았다. 생김새도 냄새도, 보지라는 이름에서 풍기는 어감 또한 꽃과는 비슷하지도 않았다. 여자의 그것은 정육점의 유리 진열장 안에 다양한 크기로 토막 난 채 진열되어 있는 고기 덩어리들과 아주 비슷했다. 표면에 흐르고 있던 끈적이는 윤기와 퀴

flower entering my body" just sounded plain weird. Was it because of its concave shape that people compared the female genitalia to a flower? Or did people mean that you could enjoy one like a flower?

The woman once saw a painting of flowers by the painter Georgia O'Keeffe. In the painting, the flowers were in full bloom, as if they were about to collapse and spill into each other like a series of conjoining, rushing rivers. They looked as if water would spring and burst off of them if you touched them with nothing more than a finger, their petals detached and open towards the black, languid gloom. Those were real flowers in full bloom—so real it was hard to believe they'd been printed on paper.

The woman suddenly lets out a sigh.

One time while the woman had been going through puberty she'd decided to look into her genitalia. Did she think it looked like a flower when she'd first carefully examined it, bowing her head and pushing a hand mirror between wide-open legs? No, she did not. The shape, smell and connotation of the term "pussy" were nothing like a

퀴한 냄새조차도. 그것이 예쁘지 않았다는 것, 예쁘기는커녕 평범하지도 않았다는 것, 기이한 열기와 뻔뻔스러운 광기까지 품고 있는 듯 보였다는 것, 때문에 사춘기 소녀였던 여자는 벽을 향해 힘껏 거울을 던질 수밖에 없었다.

거울은 어머니의 통곡 소리 같은 굉음을 내며 깨졌다.

"두 번째도, 세 번째까지도 괜찮았는데, 재 낳고 또 딸이라는 말을 들으니까 저절로 통곡이 나오더라고!"

여자의 어머니는 생각났다는 듯 말하곤 했다. 동네 아주머니들이 모여 수다를 떠는 자리에서, 명절 날 친척들이 둘러앉은 밥상머리에서, 식구들끼리 텔레비전 앞에 앉아 연속극 속에 빠져들다가, 어머니는 네 번째 딸인 여자를 손가락으로 가리키면서, 마치 목에 걸린 가시를 뽑아내듯 그 한마디를 툭 뱉어내곤 했다. 아직 어린 여자애에 지나지 않던 여자는, 어머니의 손가락이 자신을 향할 때마다 혼자 중얼거렸다. 나는 없다. 나는 없다. 나는 없다……. 여자는 그냥 허깨비였으므로, 어머니의 손가락은 여자의 존재를 가볍게 뚫고 지나가 머나먼 어딘가로 가 닿을 것 같았다.

어머니는 다섯 번째, 여섯 번째도 딸을 낳았지만, 큰

flower. Hers was actually quite similar to a lump of meat cut into various pieces, something that you might see displayed in a butcher's window down to its sticky gloss and pungent smell. It was not pretty at all. In fact, it was neither pretty nor ordinary. It even seemed to have a strange excitement to it, a shameless madness. Just a teenage girl at the time, she had no choice but to throw her mirror against the wall with all her strength.

The mirror shattered with a crash as loud as her mother bursting into tears.

"I was okay with the second daughter, even the third one, but when I gave birth to this one and learned it was a girl, well—naturally I began sobbing!"

The woman's mother would say this as if just remembering it for the first time. When women in the neighborhood got together to talk, at a table with relatives on a holiday, or rapt before a TV soap opera with other family members, her mother would point a finger at the woman, the fourth daughter, and make this comment, like she was picking out a fishbone from her neck. The woman, only a girl then, would mumble to herself: "I don't exist. I don't exist. I don't exist..."

소리로 울음을 터뜨리는 짓을 되풀이하지는 않았다. 어쩌면 네 번째라는 게 문제였는지도 모른다. 여자애는 4라는 숫자와 인연이 많았다. 여자애는 가을로 들어서는 어느 달 4일에 태어났으며, 처음 초등학교에 입학했을 때는 1학년 4반으로 배정을 받았다. 반 아이들은 4라는 숫자가 재수 없다며 투덜댔다. 여자애는 아무에게도 자기가 넷째 딸이라는 것, 네 번째 날에 태어났다는 것을 말하지 않았다. 4라는 숫자를 볼 때마다 여자애는 자기 이마에 비밀스럽게 찍혀 있는 낙인과 마주친 듯한 체념 섞인 반가움을 느꼈다.

그때 아직 어린 여자애에 지나지 않던 여자는, 언제나 고개를 숙인 채 땅바닥을 보며 걸었다. 여자는 또래 아이들보다 몸집이 컸고, 사람들의 눈길을 끄는 일이 거의 없는 아이이기도 했다. 몸집이 큰 여자애는 늘 자기 몸과 그 위에 얹혀 있는 머리가 무겁고 부담스럽기만 했다. 동작이 굼뜨고, 움직이는 것을 싫어했기에 여자애의 몸은 나날이 더 불어났다. 누구에게나 할 말이 별로 없던 여자애는, 사람들이 많은 자리에 서면, 자기 몸이 갑자기 부풀어 오르는 듯한 느낌이 들었다.

"생긴 것은 갈 데 없이 머슴애인 것이, 머리도 좋

She felt like nothing more than a ghost at times like that, believing her mother's finger could easily pass through her and reach somewhere very distant inside of her.

Though her mother would go on to give birth to a fifth and a sixth daughter, she did not repeat her bout of excessive weeping. The problem had to do with the number four, something the girl had a strong connection with. She was born on the fourth day of a month in the beginning of autumn, and was put in the fourth class when she started elementary school. Her classmates complained that the number four was unlucky. The girl never told anyone that she was the fourth daughter of the family and was born on the fourth day of the month. Whenever she saw the number four, she felt a certain sense of abandoned joy, like she'd encountered the same stigma she'd secretly branded her own forehead with.

At the time, the woman always walked with her head down, her sights set on the earth below her. She was bigger than other children her age. Her head was especially big—disproportionately big—but it rarely drew anyone's attention. She always felt that her head was as heavy as it was burden-

고…… 물건 하나만 턱 달고 나왔으면, 얼마나 좋았을 꼬……"

큰 이모는 여자애를 볼 때마다 중얼거렸다. 그런 말을 들을 때마다 여자애는 짧은 파마머리에 두부처럼 희고 말랑한 살결을 가진 이모가 차라리 다른 사람이었으면 좋겠다고 생각해버리려 했고, 하지만 눈앞에서 화장품 냄새를 생생하게 풍기고 있는 사람을 두고 그 사람이 아니었으면 좋겠다는 생각을 하는 것은 어쩐지 미안했으므로, 그냥 자기만 혼자 자기가 아닌 다른 사람이면 편하겠다는 생각을 했고, 그것 또한 누군가에게 미안해야 할 일이 아닌가 하는 생각이 들었지만, 무엇인가를 생각하고 또 생각하는 것 자체가 복잡하고 불편했으므로, 그것을 그냥 마음속에 구겨 넣어두었다.

마음속에 구겨 넣은 생각이 자꾸 꿈틀거릴 때에는, 아직 어린 여자애였던 여자는 이따금 팬티 속에 손을 집어넣어, 반드시 있어야만 했으나 자기에게는 없는, 그 무엇을 찾아 헤맸다. 아직 거웃이 나지 않은 팬티 속의 그것은 살집이 도독했으며, 부드러웠다. 잠 안 오는 밤이면, 어린 여자애는 말랑말랑한 밀가루 반죽 같은 그것을 아주 오랫동안 매만지곤 했다. 그러면 온몸이 나

some. Her movements were lethargic (she hated moving around often), so her body, day by day, grew larger and larger. The girl who did not have much to say to anyone was not comfortable with her body, which she felt swelled up suddenly in the presence of many other people.

Whenever her oldest maternal aunt saw her, she'd mumble, "She looks like a boy and she's smart... How nice would it have been if she'd been born with, you know, one of *those*...?

Every time she heard that said about her, the girl wished that her aunt—a woman with a short perm and skin as soft and white as fresh block of tofu—were someone else. But then she'd start to feel bad that she had wished that the person in front of her, whose scent of cosmetics was quite strong, should be anyone but her aunt. This would then make her think that it would be better if she were someone else entirely. But, inevitably, this would just make her think how she would probably feel bad for that person, too. In the end, she would discard all thoughts; racking her brain that much about anything was strenuous and unpleasant.

When those discarded thoughts began to surface again, though, she would slide a hand down into

른해지면서 몸 안에서 무엇인가 일렁이기 시작했다. 처음에는 그냥 오줌이 마려운 것 같았다. 하지만 시간이 흐를수록 그 느낌은 조금 복잡해졌다. 마치 사이다 속에 있는 공기 방울들이 여자애의 몸 여기저기서 터지는 듯했다. 간지럽기도 하고, 짜릿하기도 하고, 들척지근하기도 한 느낌이었다. 이상하게도 그것을 한 번 만지기 시작하면, 손의 움직임을 멈추기가 힘들었다. 야릇한 느낌은 어딘가를 향해, 무엇인가를 찾아, 끝없이 줄달음치며 솟구쳐 오르려 했고, 물통 속에 물이 차오르듯 서서히 차올라, 마침내 흘러넘치지 않으면 안 될 듯 출렁거리기 시작했다. 그러나 흘러넘칠 길을 찾지 못했던 여자애는 늘 돌파구를 찾아 쫓기듯 허덕여야 했다.

"언니, 그거 만지고 있지?"

식은땀까지 흘리면서 몸을 배배 꼬고 있는 여자애를 보면서, 한 이불을 덮고 자고 있던 동생이 소곤거렸다. 동생의 말이 채 끝나기도 전에, 아니 동생이 깨어 있다는 것을 알아차린 바로 그 순간에 여자애는 머릿속이 하얘지는 것 같았다. 그냥 옷 위로 조금 만져보았을 뿐이야, 옷 속에 손을 집어넣거나 하지는 않았어……라고 여자애는 변명하려고 했다. 차마 입에서 나오지 못

her panties in search of what she did not, but was supposed to have. That thing without pubic hair was plump and soft. On sleepless nights, she would touch this object, as soft as a small lump of dough, for a while. Her whole body would become limp and pliant and something would start to rise and swell inside her. At first, it felt like she had to go to the bathroom. But as time wore on, this feeling became ever more complicated. It was as if bubbles from a soft drink were fizzling throughout her body. It was tickling, tingling, and somewhat sweet. Oddly, it was hard to stop moving her hands once she started touching herself. A queer feeling was constantly rising to something somewhere. It intensified slowly, like water filling a bathtub. Finally, it would begin around, as if it had to overflow. Yet the girl never found a way to let herself overflow; she always felt like she was being chased by some unknown entity as she searched for a breakthrough to her problem.

"You're touching it, aren't you?" the girl's younger sister whispered.

The little girl was wriggling this way and that—sweating, actually—both she and her younger sister under the same covers on the floor. At the very

한 그 말이 전부 거짓은 아니었다. 자기 몸이긴 했지만, 두려움 때문에 결코 손을 대지 못하는 부분이 있었던 것이다.

"엄마한테 이를 거야."

동생은 모로 돌아누우며 앙칼지게 말했다. 그것은 언니인 여자애가 동생을 으를 때 하던 말이기도 했다. 동생은 아버지의 웃옷 주머니에서 몰래 동전을 꺼내어 눈깔사탕을 사 먹거나, 인형 옷을 만든답시고 어머니의 한복 치마를 가위로 오려내곤 했다. 언제나 어린 동생을 위협하던 것은 여자애였다. 하지만 이제는 입장이 바뀌어 동생의 입에서 같은 말이 흘러나왔다. 하지만 그 속에는 단순한 위협보다 더 심한 경멸이 담겨 있었다. 네가 네 몸을 만진 것은 내가 남의 물건에 손을 댄 것보다 더 나쁜 짓이라고 선언하고 있었다. 그렇기 때문에 동생은 차마 여자애의 일을 고자질할 수조차 없을지도 몰랐다. 사람들 앞에서 해서는 안 되는 말, 입에 함부로 담아서는 안 되는 말을 어머니 앞에서 소리를 내어 말해야 하기 때문에.

"난 아빠가 술집 여자랑 뽀뽀하는 것 봤다."

웬일인지 다시 돌아누운 동생이 여자애의 귀에 대고

moment that the girl realized her younger sister was awake, even before her sister had finished what she was saying, the girl was terrified. She drew a blank. She tried coming up with an excuse: she had only touched its dry parts, she'd neither inserted her fingers into the wet, warm part nor stroked or rubbed it. The words she wanted to say aloud but could not bring herself to utter were, in fact, not total lies. Even though it was her own body, there were parts that she could never touch out of fear.

"I'm gonna tell Mom on you," her younger sister hissed, then whirling around to face the other way.

The little girl used to threaten her sister. Her younger sister would steal money from their father's jacket to buy candy, or cut sections out of her mother's *hanbok* so that she could dress up her dolls. It was always the girl who threatened her younger sister. Now the tables had turned, and the words had come from her younger sister's mouth. But there was something more in her sister's tone than a mere threat. She was insinuating that touching your own body was worse than stealing. This meant there was a chance the younger sister might not tell their mother what the little girl did, as doing

속삭였다. 여자애는 갑자기 누군가 자기 뺨을 철썩 때린 것 같았다. 아버지는 집에서 얼굴을 보기 힘든 사람이었고, 어쩌다 집에 있을 때도 말이 없었으며, 늘 무표정했다. 하지만 여자애의 상상 속에서 아버지는 좋은 사람이었다. 언제나 악을 쓰고, 회초리를 휘두르며, 아이들을 모두 고아원에 갖다 버리겠다고 위협하는 어머니와는 전혀 다른 사람이었다. 게다가 드러내놓고 표현하지 않을 뿐이지, 아버지는 여섯이나 되는 딸들 가운데 자기를 가장 사랑하고 있다고 여자애는 믿고 있었다. 그렇지 않다면, 왜 유독 여자애의 성적표를 손님들 앞에서 자랑하겠는가. 아버지는 딸들의 손 한 번 잡는 법 없었고, 머리 한 번 쓰다듬어준 적이 없었지만, 여자애가 내미는 성적표를 볼 때는 입가에 엷은 미소를 띨 때도 있었다.

어느 날 골목 어귀에서 여자애는 아버지의 뒷모습을 보았다. 붉은 저녁놀 아래 아버지는 홀로 긴 그림자를 끌고 걸어가고 있었다. 사람들은 여자애가 아버지를 많이 닮았다고 했고, 그것은 하필이면 세 번째가 아니라 네 번째가 되어 버린 딸에게 매우 위안이 되는 말이기도 했다. 그래서 여자애는 와락 아버지의 팔에 매달렸

that would require her to say something out loud that was not supposed to be said in front of others, something that was never supposed to be spoken aloud, even casually.

"I saw Dad kiss a barmaid," the girl's younger sister whispered now, turning over again to the girl's side for some reason. The girl blushed. It felt like someone had suddenly slapped her. It was rare that they saw their father at home. The few times he was home he was quiet, and never with a decipherable facial expression. But in the girl's imagination her father was a good person. He was completely different from their mother, who was always shouting at her daughters, whipping them with a rod, or telling them to do this or that. Of the six daughters, the girl believed that her father loved her the most, even if he did not show his affection openly. If that were not the case, she reasoned, why would he sometimes show off her report card to guests? Her father never held hands with his daughters or patted them on the head, but sometimes a faint smile would tug at the corners of his mouth upon looking at the little girl's report card.

One time in the early evening she saw her father's back at the entrance of a lane to their house. He

던 것인지도 모른다. 아버지의 짙은 잿빛 그림자 위로 자기 마음속에 구겨 넣어둔 복잡한 생각의 한 자락이 펼쳐지기를 바라면서. 하지만 어쩌면 좋은 사람일지도 모른다고 생각했던 아버지는 무표정한 얼굴로 매몰차게 여자애의 손길을 뿌리쳤다.

어느 여름날의 기억이 떠오르면서 여자애의 아랫배가 싸늘해졌다. 토할 것 같았다. 그 여름날, 아버지는 대청마루의 돗자리 위에 누워 낮잠을 자고 있었다. 여자애는 아버지 곁에 얌전히 누웠다. 아늑하고 편안했다. 한 뼘쯤 떨어진 곳에 누워 있는 아버지에게서 땀냄새와 뒤섞인 담배 냄새를 맡을 수 있었고, 그 냄새는 어쩐지 달콤했다. 여자애는 고개를 돌려 아버지의 하얀 손등 위에 살짝 새끼손가락을 대보기도 했다. 아버지의 손가락은 하얗고 길었고, 가끔 그 손가락으로 이상한 글씨가 가득 씌어 있는 책장을 넘기기도 했으며, 전축 위에 검고 동그란 판을 얹고 아주 지루한 음악을 들으며 오랫동안 앉아 있기도 했다.

"넌 여기서 뭐하는 거야?"

설핏 잠이 들었는가 싶었을 때, 아버지의 짜증스러운 목소리가 느닷없이 여자애의 얼굴을 향해 쏟아졌다. 어

was walking alone under the evening glow, a long shadow trailing behind him. People said the girl resembled her father a lot. That provided her, the fourth—not the third—daughter, with a great deal of comfort. Perhaps, that was why she had abruptly ran to him and latched on to his arm, hoping that some of her disjointed thoughts that ran rampant in her mind would spread themselves out over the dark grey shadow of her father. Although she had always thought of her father as a good person, he had shaken her roughly off of him.

This brought to mind a certain summer's day, which made her lower abdomen turn cold. She felt like vomiting. That day her father had been napping on a bamboo mat in the common room of the house. The girl had noiselessly lain down beside her father. She was cozy and comfortable, and could smell her father's sweat mixed in with the scent of cigarette smoke just inches away. The smell was warm and sweet. The girl turned her face so that she was touching the back of her father's white hand with her pinky. He had long, white fingers, fingers which he occasionally used to turn the pages of a book full of strange scripts, or to put on a round black disc on the record player

느 새 일어나 있던 아버지가 누워 있는 여자애의 옆구리를 발짓으로 밀어내며 방 안으로 들어갔다. 여자애는 그대로 텅 빈 마루에 누워 있었다. 흙바닥이라고는 한 조각도 찾아볼 수 없는 마당의 콘크리트 위로 땡볕이 쏟아졌다. 땀에 젖은 여자애의 팔뚝에 소름이 돋기 시작했다. 아무도 살지 않는 빈집처럼 주위는 고요했다. 어지럼증을 느끼며 일어나, 여자애는 대문을 열고 집 앞 골목으로 나왔다. 지나가는 강아지 한 마리도 보이지 않는 골목에는 보도블록들이 백열등처럼 하얗게 빛나고 있었다. 여자애는 주먹을 꼭 쥔 채 울퉁불퉁한 시멘트 담벼락을 손등으로 긁으며 걸었다. 손등이 까져 쓰리고 아팠다. 여자애는 텅 빈 골목길을 자꾸자꾸 걸었다. 더 이상 아픔을 참을 수 없었을 때 여자애는 걸음을 멈추고 쓰린 손등을 혀로 핥았다. 시멘트 가루 냄새와 피비린내가 콧속을 파고들었고, 울컥 올라오는 구역질과 함께 여자애는 뱃속에 든 것을 게워냈다. 뜨거운 담벼락을 붙들고 토악질을 하는 여자애의 눈앞에 어둡고 텅 빈 구멍이 어른거리고 있었다.

아니, 그건 아니었다. 벽에 던져진 거울이 정말로 깨진 것은 아니었다. 아직 사춘기 소녀였던 여자는, 바닥

so he could sit for hours listening to boring music.

"What are you doing here?" her father asked abruptly, irritated. His words had assaulted her as she'd drifted in and out of sleep. Before she knew it, he was awake. Then he pushed the girl away with his feet and walked into his room while she remained lying on the barren floor. The blazing sun shone upon the cement in the front yard, where not a single grain of soil was present. Her forearms, damp with sweat, broke out into a rash of goose bumps. The house was silent, like it was uninhabited and empty. The girl stood up, feeling dizzy, and then opened the front gate and walked out to the lane in front of her house. On a lane where one couldn't even see a small dog, the street blocks shone as white as a line of lamps. The girl walked down the lane, scratching the rough cement wall with a firmly clenched fist. The back of her hand was grazed and felt sore. She continued walking along the empty lane. When she could not stand the pain any longer, she stopped and licked the back of her burning hand with her tongue. She could smell cement and dust and blood. Suddenly, she threw up. While she was vomiting, leaning her hand against the hot summer day's wall, a dark, va-

에 떨어진 거울을 집어 들고 다시 한 번 다리를 벌려 안쪽 깊숙한 곳을 들여다보았다. 결코 꽃처럼 예쁘지 않은 그것은 아무리 들여다봐도 싫증이 나지 않을 만큼 섬뜩하게 낯설었다. 물론 소녀의 주위에는 아무도 없었다. 자기 몸을 만지다가 동생에게 들킨 다음부터, 혼자 집을 보는 날처럼, 아무에게도 들키지 않을 상황이 아니면, 소녀는 절대로 그런 짓을 하지 않았다. 그것은 자신에게도, 그 장면을 목격하게 될 상대방에게도 재앙에 가까운 일이라는 것을 깨달았으므로.

거울을 통해 자신의 몸의 낯선 부위를 들여다보다가, 소녀는 처음으로 자기 몸에 있는 구멍을 볼 수 있었다. 얼마 전 호기심으로 구입한 삽입형 생리대를 사용해보려고 했을 때, 끝내 찾지 못했던 구멍이었다. 겹겹의 살덩이에 둘러싸인 그것은 구멍이라기보다는 길게 찢어져 열려 있는 상처처럼 보였으며, 무엇인가 조금만 닿아도 금방 핏물이 배어나올 듯했다. 소녀는 감히 그 구멍 속에 손가락 굵기의 생리대를 집어넣을 용기가 나지 않았다. 구멍 근처까지 생리대를 가져가보기는 했지만, 갑자기 몸이 굳어지면서 다리가 떨렸다. 소녀는 보지 말았어야 할 것을 보고 말았다는 후회에 사로잡혔다.

cant hole wavered before the girl's eyes.

No, it really did not happen. The mirror she threw against the wall had not actually broken. The woman, who was then only a teenager, picked the mirror up off the floor and looked deep inside her open legs once again. What was never as pretty as a flower was so astonishingly unfamiliar that she did not get tired of looking into it. Of course, there was nobody around her at the time. After her younger sister had caught her touching herself, the girl never repeated this behavior except when she could be certain no one would discover her, like when she was alone at home. Otherwise, she knew it would be a disaster not only for her, but also for the person who had caught her.

As she was looking into that strange part of her body with the mirror, the girl found the opening in her body for the first time. It was an opening she had searched for in vain some days before when she'd tried to use a tampon that she had just bought out of curiosity. This thing surrounded by so many folds of flesh looked like a long, torn scar rather than just a hole, as if it would ooze blood if anything even grazed it. She did not dare to insert a tampon as thick as a finger into it. She brought it

아무도 없는 골목길에서 피비린내를 맡으며 토악질을 하던 기억이 떠올랐다.

그 이후로 소녀는 다리 사이에 다시 거울을 들이대지는 않았지만, 구멍의 존재를 머릿속에서 완전히 지울 수는 없었다. 소녀는 엄마나 언니, 학교 친구들 그리고 거리를 걸어가는 날씬한 미니스커트의 여자들을 볼 때마다, 그들의 치마 속에 존재할 기괴한 구멍들을 떠올리곤 했다. 웃음이 터질 것 같으면서도 동시에 온몸에 소름이 돋아나는 일이었다.

그 무렵 여자는 하이틴 로맨스나 할리퀸 문고 같은 연애 소설에 푹 빠져 있었다. 소설 속에 나오는 입맞춤이며 포옹, 애무 같은 성행위에 대한 온갖 묘사들을 읽으면서, 아직 덜 자란 소녀였고 따라서 섹스를 경험하지 못했던 여자는 섹스에 대해 분홍색 구름 같은 기대를 품었다. 파도 거품 속에서 태어난 비너스처럼 풍만하고 미끈한 여자와 단단한 근육질의 남자가 서로의 몸을 부드럽게 어루만질 때, 천국에서나 맛볼 수 있는 황홀함으로 심장이 터져나갈 것 같으리라고 소녀는 상상했다. 한 몸이 된 남자와 여자 주위로 무지갯빛 안개가 내려앉으며, 연꽃처럼 커다란 꽃으로 피어나게 될지도

close to the opening but suddenly her body stiffened and her legs began to shake. She seized up with regret at the thought that she'd seen something she shouldn't have. This brought her back to the day when she was all alone in the lane outside her home and had smelled the blood that had made her vomit.

She had not pushed a mirror down between her legs since then. And yet she could never erase the image from her mind. The girl was reminded of these strange openings inside women's skirts whenever she saw her mother, her sisters, friends from school—even the thin girls wearing miniskirts on the streets. It made her want to burst out laughing. It also gave her goose bumps all over her body.

When she was in her teens, the woman was fascinated by teenage romance stories. After reading about all sorts of stories with sex and foreplay, she—still not fully developed and so had not had sex yet—grew to anticipate that sex would be like a pink cloud. She imagined that a glamorous, sleek woman like Venus, born from the bubbles of waves, and a strong, chiseled man would gently caress each other's bodies, their hearts ready to

모른다고 생각했다. 사춘기 소녀의 분홍색 구름 같은 기대 속에서 섹스는 꽃처럼 활짝 피어나는 순간이었다. 하지만 남자와 여자가 어떤 방식으로 교접하는지 잘 알고 있었음에도, 이상하게도 소녀는 자기 몸에 분명 존재하는 구멍과 섹스를 연결시키지 않았다. 마치 어쩌고 저쩌고 심의위원회에서 영화를 검열하듯, 소녀가 상상하는 지나치게 열정적이어서 슬프기까지 한 섹스의 장면에는 성기의 접촉이 결코 등장하지 않았다. 꽃처럼 활짝 피어나는 섹스에 비해 구멍이란 너무 습하고 어두운 것이었으니까.

밤늦게 학교에서 집으로 돌아오던 어느 날, 좁은 골목길을 지나다가 소녀는 뒤에서 다가온 검은 그림자에게 목이 졸렸다. 그리고 땅에 나자빠지고 말았다. 검은 그림자는 잠시 머뭇거리더니, 소녀의 뒤집혀진 치마 속으로 손을 집어넣었다. 정신을 차린 소녀가 들고 있던 책가방으로 검은 그림자를 힘껏 때리면서 소리를 지르자, 서툰 손길로 소녀의 허벅지를 더듬던 검은 그림자는 벌떡 일어나 소녀에게 발길질을 하기 시작했다. 소녀의 비명 소리에 이어 어디선가 들려오는 사람들의 발자국 소리에 검은 그림자는 허둥지둥 사라져버렸다. 아주 짧

burst with heavenly ecstasy. She thought that a rainbow-colored mist might also descend upon the man and woman, who had became one by this point and reached a magnificent bloom like a lotus flower. That was it—sex was a moment of blooming, like a flower, the anticipation of an adolescent girl lying hidden among a pink cloud. However, though she knew how a man and woman had sexual intercourse, strangely enough she could not connect sex with the opening that existed in her own body. She imagined sex as both passionate and sad, an act where there was never any contact between the genitals. It was as if it had been censored by a committee, like one of those censored movies; the opening was too dark, damp, and dangerous to compare sex with the blooming of a flower.

Once, when she was coming back home from school late at night, she was strangled by a black shadow that approached her from behind on a narrow lane. When she collapsed to the ground, the black shadow momentarily hesitated, then pushed his hand up the girl's upturned skirt. Using her school bag, she hit the black shadow with all her strength. She screamed out loud after she

은 순간이었지만, 소녀는 죽음의 공포를 느꼈다. 그리고 강간이 단지 억지로 성관계를 맺는 정도의 사건이 아니라는 사실을 깨달았다. 강간은 무참하게 얻어맞은 끝에, 한 사람, 하나의 인격체는 사라지고, 그저 하나의 구멍만 존재하게 되는 일이었다. 그 일이 있고 난 후, 종종 소녀는 산부인과를 찾아가 자신의 구멍을 막아달라는 부탁을 하고 싶다는 충동에 사로잡혔다. 다리 사이에 있는 구멍 하나 때문에 맞아 죽을 수도 있다는 사실을 알게 되었으므로.

벽에 그려진 꽃에서 눈길을 거둔 여자는 오른쪽 옆으로 고개를 돌린다. 벌거벗은 등이 있다. 움츠러든 좁은 어깨와 하나하나 세어볼 수 있을 정도로 드러난 척추의 마디, 길고 가는 허리가 눈에 들어온다. 아직 사춘기 소녀였던 여자가 꿈꾸던 구릿빛 근육질의 몸과는 거리가 멀다. 물론 벌거벗은 야윈 등을 훑어보고 있는 여자의 몸 또한, 파도 거품 속에서 태어난 비너스와는 비슷하지도 않다. 여자는 여전히 자신의 몸이 지닌 부피와 형태가 거북하다. 여자는 몸을 돌려 벌거벗은 등의 야윈

gathered herself together. The black shadow, who until then was clumsily fumbling with her thighs, suddenly stood up and started to kick the girl. Soon, there was the sound of people approaching, and the black shadow hastily disappeared. Although the encounter had been brief, the girl had been momentarily afraid of dying, and realized that rape wasn't just sex by force. Rape was something where, after someone was savagely beaten, a person or a person's character disappeared, and all that existed was a gaping opening, a hole. After her own run-in with the black shadow, the girl was seized with the impulse to have a gynecologist cover her hole. She understood now that she could be beaten to death because of its existence.

The woman stops looking at the flowers painted on the wall. She turns her head to the right, where she sees a man's naked back. She looks at his long, slim waist, the narrowed shoulders and joints of his spine that are revealed so clearly she can count them one by one. This was far from the tanned, muscular body that the woman dreamt of when she was a teenager. Then again, the body of the woman scrutinizing the thin naked back is in no way

몸을 감싸 안는다. 흐물흐물한 여자의 뱃살이 벌거벗은 등의 단단한 척추에 닿는다. 여자는 앞으로 손을 뻗어, 조금 전까지 자신의 몸 안에 머물렀던 벌거벗은 등의 성기를 만져본다. 차갑고 부드럽다.

여자는 발기한 남자의 성기를 처음 보았을 때를 떠올린다. 신촌의 어느 지하 다방에서였다. 그 다방 한쪽 구석에는 원래 하나의 공간이었던 곳을 무리하게 복층으로 개조한 곳이 있었다. 천장이 낮은 탓에 앉아 있기도 불편해서, 아래층에 자리가 없을 때에도 사람들이 이층으로 올라가기를 꺼렸다. 스무 살 무렵의 여자는, 늘 텅텅 비어 있는 그 어두컴컴한 이층에서 처음 사귀기 시작한 남자친구와 하릴없이 시간을 보낼 때가 많았다. 그날도 마찬가지였다. 음악을 듣고, 수다를 떨고, 낙서를 했다. 그리고 입맞춤을 했고, 서로의 옷 속으로 손을 집어넣었다. 남자는 이따금 자신의 바지 안으로 들어와 있는 여자의 손목을 쥐고 어떻게 손을 움직여야 하는지 자세히 가르쳐주었다. 여자는 손에 쥐고 있는 것이 점점 단단해지고 뜨거워지는 것을 느꼈다. 좁고 답답한 허리춤에서 손을 꺼내면서 여자는 남자에게 말했다.

"보여줘. 보고 싶어."

similar to the Venus born from the bubbles of waves. The woman still feels uncomfortable about the size and shape of her body. She turns and embraces the naked back's thin frame. The saggy flesh of her belly touches its strong spine. The woman now reaches her hand to the front and touches the genital member, which was in her until just a moment ago. It is now cold and soft.

The woman recalls the first time she saw a man's erect genitalia. It was at an underground coffee shop in the Sinchon area. One corner of the shop had been, it seemed, abruptly renovated into two floors. It was uncomfortable to sit on the top level because of the low ceiling, and people hesitated to go up there even when there were no seats left on the first floor. The woman, then around the age of twenty, often spent her free time with her first boyfriend on the dark, empty second floor. It was the same that day, too. They'd listened to music, chatted, and scribbled some drawings. Then they'd kissed and put their hands under each other's clothing. Sometimes the man taught her carefully how to move her hand in his pants by holding her wrist. What she held in her hand became increasingly hotter and harder. After removing her hand

잠깐 머뭇거리던 남자는 바지 지퍼를 내리고 발기한 성기를 꺼냈다. 주위는 어두웠으나, 두 사람의 머리 위에 매달려 있던 작은 램프 불빛이 스포트라이트처럼 그것을 비추었다. 여자는 가늘고 푸른 정맥이 도드라져 보이는 남자의 불그레한 성기를 보고 조금 놀랐다. 그리고 조금 두려움을 느꼈다. 당황하며 고개를 돌리다가 남자와 눈이 마주쳤을 때, 여자는 또 한 번 놀랐다. 남자의 눈빛은 낯선 열기로 흐려져 있었으나, 한편으로는 자랑스러움을 내보이며 반짝이고 있었기 때문이다. 여자는 자신의 몸을 타인에게 내보이면서 한 번도 자랑스러움을 느껴본 적이 없었다. 얼굴을 똑바로 들고 거리를 걷는 일도 때로는 힘겨웠다. 아무도 없는 방에서 조심스럽게 거울을 들이대고, 스스로의 몸을 들여다볼 때도 여자를 지배했던 것은 모욕감과 수치스러움이었다.

어느 겨울 여자는 연안 부두에서 남자와 함께 배에 올라탔다. 첫 섹스를 섬에서 하고 싶다는 막연한 바람 때문이었다. 섬은 여자가 한 번도 가보지 못한 곳이었다. 어쩌면 여자가 선택한 것은 '섬'이라는 이름에 숨어

from the narrow, constraining waist area of his pants, the woman said to the man, "Show it to me. I want to see it."

The man was reluctant for a second. Then he lowered his zipper and took it out. Everything was dark expect for a tiny lamp over their heads that highlighted his genitalia. The woman was a little taken aback at the reddish object that clearly had fine blue veins running along its surface. She was also a little scared. Confused, she turned her head and met his eyes. The woman was again surprised to see that the man's eyes were bleary with a strange kind of excitement that also shone with a great pride. The woman never felt proud when she showed her body to others. Sometimes it was hard enough just walking down the street with her head held up at eye level. Even when there was no one else in the room with her, it was disgust and shame that ruled over her when she angled the mirror to look at her body.

One winter's day, she took a boat to an island with the intention of having sex for the first time. She had never been to an island before. Perhaps the reason she chose an island had something to

있는 아련함과 모호함의 힘이었는지도 몰랐다. 한겨울의 높은 파도는 갑판 밑 딱딱한 마룻바닥에 앉아 있던 여자를 멀미에 시달리게 만들었다. 어지럼과 메스꺼움에 지친 몸으로 겨우 발을 내딛은 땅은, 그러나, 쓸쓸하고 황량했다. 여자의 머릿속에 들어 있던 섬은, 마치 벽에 걸린 달력에서 빠져나온 듯 끝없이 펼쳐진 흰 모래밭에 파란 파도가 넘실대는 열대의 어느 곳이었던 것 같다. 배에서 내리자마자 여자는 짙은 잿빛 개펄 위에 흩어져 있는 썩어가는 로프와 흰 스티로폼 조각들, 조각난 그물, 플라스틱 막걸리 통들로 가득한 섬과 만났다. 콧속으로 파고드는 비린 갯내를 맡았을 때 여자는 배의 갑판 밑에 앉아 있을 때보다 더 심한 멀미를 느꼈다. 그대로 돌아가고 싶었지만, 하루에 한 번 다닌다는 배는 이미 바다 한가운데로 자취를 감춘 뒤였다. 여자는 말없이 걸어가는 남자의 뒤를 따랐다. 방파제를 따라 걷던 남자는 육중한 몸체를 서로 얽은 채 쌓여 있는 삼발이 위로 훌쩍 올라섰다. 한겨울의 쌀쌀한 날씨 탓인지 낚시꾼들조차 보이지 않았다.

아직 앳된 얼굴의 여자와 남자를 아래위로 훑어보던 낚시 가게 주인의 눈길을 뒤통수에 느끼며, 두 사람은

do with its unknown power that she knew nothing about. As she lay on the hard wooden floor under the deck, the motion of the high waves of the winter sea made the woman seasick. When she finally managed to stand on land again she was exhausted. The image she had always had of an island was of a tropical locale with endless white sand and rolling blue waves, some place you might see on a calendar. The island that greeted her as soon as she got off the ship, however, was lonely and desolate. Withered ropes, ragged hunks of Styrofoam, broken nets, and plastic bottles of crude rice wine dotted the dark grey mudflats. Her seasickness now felt worse than when she was sitting under the deck of the ship. She wanted to go back home right away, but the ship only made the trip once a day, and had already disappeared back out to sea. The woman followed the man, who walked on in silence. He was walking along the breakwater structure and he stepped up on the piled tetrapods, their heavy bodies interlocked with one another. There was no fisherman anywhere, probably because the weather was so cold.

Feeling the glance of a fishing store owner at the back of their heads, the couple looked back. The

낚시 가게 뒷방으로 스며들 듯 몸을 숨겼다. 낯선 사람의 체취가 물씬 풍기는 이불을 앞에 놓고 앉아서, 여자는 잠깐 지하 다방의 밀폐된 공기를 그리워했다. 아귀가 맞지 않는 미닫이문 틈새로 찬바람은 끊임없이 불어 들어왔고, 바람에 뒤섞여 두런두런 이야기를 나누는 사람들의 목소리도 함께 따라 들어왔다. 양철 판으로 막아놓은 미닫이문 저쪽에 몇몇 사람들이 모여 있는 것 같았다. 처음에는 낮은 웅얼거림이었던 말소리들은, 넋두리 비슷한 노랫가락으로 변하더니, 어느 순간 내지르는 술주정으로 변해가고 있었다.

그때 여자는 자꾸만 힘이 들어가는 남자의 손길을 뿌리치고 있었다. 남자의 손길은 이제 거의 폭력으로 느껴졌으나, 여자는 도저히 옷을 벗을 수 없었다. 낯설고 불안하고 두렵기만 했다. 언제 문이 벌컥 열릴지 알 수 없었다. 남자는 짜증을 부리고 성을 냈다. 바깥에서 들려오는 목소리도 점점 더 거세고 높아졌다. 술주정은 말다툼으로 변했고, 바닷바람은 양철 판을 부술 것 같은 기세로 불어오고 있었다.

여자가 기대했던 분홍빛 구름 같은 첫 섹스는 없었다. 기억나는 것은 진저리나는 구멍 찾기뿐이었다. 남자에

owner looked the man and woman—young enough to be his kids—up and down. The couple hid themselves in the backroom of the fishing shop, which also doubled as a small inn.

The woman sat in front of a pile of comforters. They were folded on the floor and reeked of the people who had last used them The woman momentarily longed for the stuffy air of the underground coffee shop. A cold wind kept passing through the chink in the sliding door whose wooden frame did not fit securely. The sound of people talking nearby mixed with the sound of the wind. It seemed as if several people had gathered near the narrow wooden floor over by the door. Their voices, which came through as a low mumble at first, grew into a grumbling and eventually turned into drunken, frenzied yelling. The woman was pushing away the man's hands now, which were groping at her with increasing urgency. His hands felt almost violent now, though she could not possibly take her clothes off. It felt strange being there, and she was filled with a sense of fear and anxiousness. She had no idea if or when the door would open. The man suddenly grew irritated and angry. The voices outside also became wilder

게도 첫 경험인 섹스였으므로, 그는 식은땀을 흘리며, 여자의 거웃과 살덩이들을 헤집었다. 거의 해부학적인 관심에 가까운 탐구였다. 마침내 여자의 다리는 제법 큰 원을 그리기 위한 컴퍼스의 다리처럼 벌어졌고, 남자는 삽입을 시도했다. 어쩌면 어느 순간까지 여자는 남자에게 따뜻하기도 하고 상냥하기도 한 감정을 기대했는지도 모른다. 하지만 우스꽝스럽고 불편한 자세로 누워 있는 여자와 그 앞에 선 남자의 모습에서는, 따뜻함일 수도 있고 상냥함일 수도 있으며, 분홍빛 구름이거나 무지갯빛 안개일 수도 있는 그 무엇의 흔적은 찾아볼 수 없었다. 남자는 모든 것을 잊고 오로지 자신의 성기를 구멍에 집어넣는 일에 열중했다. 남자 자신도 그 자리에서 사라졌고, 오직 단단한 그것만이 남았다. 그것은 열심히 구멍을 찾았고, 그 속에 자신을 집어넣었으며, 파국을 향해 허겁지겁 돌진했다. 그 모든 과정을 거치고 난 후에야 다시 원래의 모습인 사람으로 돌아올 수 있다는 듯이.

"더러워."

다시 사람으로 돌아온 남자가 내뱉은 첫마디였다.

"고상한 척, 잘난 척은 혼자 다 하더니. 냄새도 지독하

and higher pitched. The drunken, frenzied voice outside sounded argumentative now. Meanwhile, the wind blowing in off the sea was so strong that it seemed it would soon destroy the tin panel that covered the sliding glass door.

Her first time having sex was nothing like the pink cloud she had envisioned in her youth. What she remembered was an awful search for the hole. It was the man's first time too, so he searched for it through the woman's mass of flesh, from her pubic hair, labia majora, and labia minora, to the vagina itself. It was an exploration on the man's part, almost like he was pursuing some sort of item of anatomical interest. At last, the woman's legs spread open, like the legs of a compass prepared to draw a giant circle, and the man tried to insert himself into her. She might have expected some amount of warmth and kindness from the man—for at least part of it. But in the end there was no sign of anything that one could call warmth or kindness, pink clouds or rainbow-colored mist between the man in front of her and the woman lying awkwardly on the floor. He thought of nothing else as he concentrated on the job of inserting himself into her hole. The man himself had disappeared; only this

고……."

밖에서 갑자기 병이 깨지는 소리가 났다. 누군가 절규에 가까운 울음을 터뜨렸고, 발로 차이고 주먹으로 얻어맞는 소리가 들려왔다. 욕설과 비명과 가라앉지 않는 흐느낌이, 바람에 흔들리는 시끄러운 양철 판 소리와 함께, 미닫이문 틈새로 소나기처럼 들이쳤다.

여자는 불두덩 뼈를 망치로 얻어맞은 듯한 아픔을 느끼며 누워 있었다. 아픔은 여자의 머릿속을 유리알처럼 차갑고 명료하게 만들었으나, 몸을 움직이고 싶지는 않았다. 여자는 그저 밖에서 들려오는 울음 섞인 젊은 남자의 넋두리에 귀를 기울일 뿐이었다.

"이렇게 살고 싶지 않아…… 개새끼들. 이 씨발 놈아…… 이렇게 썩고 싶지 않다고…… 썅…… 우리가 쓰레긴 줄 알아? 여기 그냥 처박혀 살라고? 이렇게, 평생?"

다음 날 아침 욱신거리는 몸을 이끌고 여자는 미닫이문 저쪽, 양철 판자로 닫혀 있는 낚시 가게 앞으로 가보았다. 여자는 깨진 소주병과 흩어져 있는 유리 조각들, 굴러다니는 휴지 뭉치와 신문지 몇 장을 보았다. 그럴 이유는 없었지만, 여자는 흥건히 고여 있는 핏물 같은 것을 볼 수 있으리라 기대했다. 손톱만 한 핏방울도, 말

blind, stiff member remained. It searched ardently for the opening, inserted itself into it, and rushed to catastrophe. It was almost as if it could only become human again only after it had gone through the entire process.

"Dirty." That was the first thing the man said when he became human again. "You pretended to be refined, well-behaved... and it even stinks..."

Suddenly there was the sound of a bottle being broken. Somebody burst into tears like they were screaming. There was the sound of someone being beaten. Name-calling, screams, and sobbing streamed into the backroom like a sudden shower through the chink in the door, as did the racket of the tin panel, being shaken by the wind.

The woman was lying in pain, as if the front of her pelvis had been hit with a hammer. The pain made her head as cool and clear as a glass bead, yet she did not want to move her body. She just listened to the cries from outside, which were mixed in with a young man's complaints.

"I don't want to live like this... Bastards... I don't want to be forgotten this way... Damn it... Do they think we're garbage? Do they want us to be stuck here?"

라붙은 검붉은 자국조차도 찾아볼 수 없었지만.

아직도 여자는 궁금하다. 처음으로 남자와 섹스를 했던 그때, 왜 피가 보이지 않았을까? 피는 보이지 않았으나, 며칠 동안 제대로 걸음을 걷지 못할 만큼 여자를 괴롭혔던 아픔은 무엇 때문이었을까? 자전거를 많이 타면 처녀막이 파열되는 경우도 있다는 얘기가 있지만, 여자는 자전거를 탈 줄 모른다. 거울을 들이대고 자기 몸에 있는 구멍을 찾아낸 후에도, 여자는 두려움 때문에 끝내 삽입형 생리대를 쓰지 못했다. 그렇다면 피가 비치지 않았던 것은 지나친 자위행위 때문이었을까? 하지만 자위라고 할 수 있는 행위를 하기 시작한 것은 첫 섹스를 경험한 이후였다.

남자친구와 헤어지고, 휴학을 하고, 집에 틀어박혀 있던 일 년 동안 거의 매일 여자를 사로잡았던 것은, 동네 버스 정류장 앞에 있는 '번개 전자'의 오토바이 타고 다니는 전기공 총각이었다. 여자는 총각과 짧은 인사 한 번 나눈 적이 없고, 엇갈려 지나치다가 서로 눈이 마주친 적도 없었다. 현실에서의 여자는 남자들의 관심이나

The next morning, the woman's aching body was drawn to the front of the fishing store. Above the door she saw a tin panel. Also, there were broken *soju* bottles on the ground, other random scattered pieces of glass, huge wads of tissue flying around, and a few sheets of newspaper. For no particular reason, she expected to see something like a pool of blood from the fight. But she couldn't find the tiniest drop of blood or even a dried dark red stain.

The woman is still wondering why there was no blood after having sex for the first time. None at all. She asked herself what could have caused the pain that bothered her for several days, the pain that hurt so much that it was hard to walk.

She'd heard that you could tear a hymen if you rode your bicycle too often. The woman did not know how to ride a bicycle, so it couldn't have been that. After that day when the woman had found the hole in her body by pushing a mirror up between her legs, she could not bring herself to use a tampon out of fear. Was it because of excessive masturbation that there was no blood, the woman wondered. Although, upon further reflection, she remembered that it was only after losing

시선을 끌어본 적이 별로 없으므로, 그것은 어쩌면 당연한 일이었다. 하지만 여자의 머릿속에서 번개 전자의 총각은 여자를 열렬하게 숭배했으며, 거칠고 과감한 구애를 감행하기도 했다. 어린 여자애였을 때는 몸 안을 흘러 다니는 뜨거운 느낌을 처리하지 못해 허덕이던 여자가 마침내 그 분출구를 발견했던 것이다. 뜨거운 느낌을 흘러넘치게 하려면, 말초적 감각보다는 상상력이 중요하다는 사실을 여자는 깨달았다. 상상 속에서의 여자는 파도 거품 속에서 태어난 비너스였다. 여자가 원하는 사람은 누구나 여자에게 매혹되었고, 여자는 그들을 쉽게 지배할 수 있었다. 남자들은 여자의 아름다움에 전율하며 무릎을 꿇었고, 바로 그 순간 여자도 스스로를 사랑할 수 있었으며, 온몸을 훑고 지나가는 황홀한 떨림을 느낄 수 있었다.

"이번 주에 너는 내성적이었어? 외향적이었어?"

벌거벗은 등은 이따금 여자에게 묻는다. 여자와 벌거벗은 등은 어느 책에선가 '내성적인 사람일수록 자위의 빈도가 잦다'는 글을 읽은 적이 있었다.

her virginity that she'd started masturbating at a rate that one might call excessive.

Sometime after breaking up with the man whom she had first had sex with, the woman took a year off from school. During that year off, there was an electrician in her neighborhood who captivated her attention almost every day. He rode a motorcycle with the store name, Lightning Electronics, which was located in front of a nearby bus stop. The woman had never said hello to the young man, nor did their eyes ever meet as they passed each other on the road.

For the most part, the woman rarely drew the attention of men so it seemed natural that she did not grab his attention as well. In her fantasies, though, the young man from Lightning Electronics adored her, entreating her for her love boldly and wildly. Although as a little girl she had not known what to do about the heat that would well up inside of her, she now had finally found the answer to her problem. She realized that in order to let those same burning feeling overflow, imagination was more important than the five senses. In her imagination, the woman was Venus, born from the bubbles of waves. Everyone she wanted was at-

"내가 보는 앞에서 한번 해봐. 네가 그러고 있으면, 예뻐 보일 것 같아."

여자는 피식 웃는다. 남자들이 떠올리는 여자들의 자위행위란 뻔하다. 예뻐 보인다고? 꿀배 같은 젖가슴을 드러낸 채, 아기 속살 같은 연분홍빛 성기를 보여주면서, 카메라를 향해 갈구하는 듯한 눈빛을 던지는 포르노 배우의 모습은 물론 예뻐 보일 것이다.

그러나 여자는 포르노 배우가 아니다. 포르노 배우라고 할지라도 그토록 고혹적인 모습을 연출하면서 절정에 도달할 수 있을 것인가? 다른 사람들은 어떨지 몰라도, 여자에게 자위를 해서 오르가슴에 도달할 수 있느냐의 여부는, 말초적 감각과는 상관없이, 상상에 얼마나 집중할 수 있느냐에 달려 있었다. 누군가 자신의 모습을 지켜보고 있다면, 자위를 해서 절대로 절정에 도달할 수 없을 것이라고 여자는 생각한다. 문득 여자는 궁금하다. 포르노 속의 미녀들도 상상 속에서 스스로를 다른 모습으로 바꿀 것인가? 아니면 그들에게 상상 따위는 아예 필요가 없는 것일까?

"여기, 여기, 여기를 뜯어고치면 너도 꽤 괜찮은 편이야."

tracted to her, and she could control them easily. Men were in awe of her beauty and knelt down before her. During those moments, the woman was able to love herself too, she would feel a rapturous trembling pass through her body.

"Were you introverted or extroverted this week?"

The naked back sometimes asks the woman this question. The woman and the naked back once read in a book, "the more introverted a person is, the more frequently they masturbate." Though it was not clear from what source the book was quoting, it went on to classify the number of times someone masturbated by how introverted or extroverted they were.

"Go ahead and give it a try in front of me. I bet you'd look beautiful doing it."

The woman laughs helplessly. It is clear that men have a fixed idea of what female masturbation is like. Beautiful? Of course porn stars gazing longingly at the camera, revealing their breasts like giant honey pears and showing off genitalia as pink as a baby skin might look beautiful.

She, however, is not a porn star. Even if she were, could she bring herself to a climax while

여자의 뱃살과 젖가슴과 허벅지를 손가락으로 가리키며 선심 쓰듯 말하는 벌거벗은 등은, 자위를 끝낸 뒤 여자가 돌아가야 하는 남루한 현실의 쓸쓸함 따위를 이해할 수 있을까? 상상 속에서조차 있는 그대로의 몸으로는, 여자가 결코 성적인 욕망을 느낄 수 없다는 사실을 알고 있을까?

"수컷들도 불쌍하기는 마찬가지야. 이걸 세우기 위해 얼마나 용을 써야 하는지 알아? 발기라는 건 결국 긴장을 유지하는 거라고. 발기된 상태를 계속 유지하려면, 여자보다 훨씬 잘나야 하고, 여자를 지배할 수 있어야 하고, 여자가 자기 몸 안에 이걸 집어넣어주기를 간절히 원한다는 걸 확신해야 하지."

여자는 벌거벗은 등이 말하는 발기된 상태라는 것 자체를 이해할 수 없다. 물론 여자에게도 섹스할 준비가 이루어지는 상태가 있기는 하다. 하지만 여자는 굳이 그런 상태가 되지 않아도 언제나 섹스를 할 수 있다. 여자와 남자의 가장 큰 생리적 차이점이면서, 여자가 가장 아쉬워하는 부분이기도 하다. 섹스하고 싶지 않거나, 준비가 되어 있지 않을 때, 억지로 하지 않아도 되는 장치가 여자의 몸에는 마련되어 있지 않다.

showing off that sort of seductive figure? She can't speak for anyone else, but for her it would depend upon whether she could focus on her dreams and fantasies, not on things like vibrators or dildos stimulating her senses. She doesn't think that she could ever reach climax masturbating if somebody were watching her. Suddenly the woman wonders —do all those porn actresses become someone else in their imagination? Or do they not need any imagination at all?

"You'd look all right if you could fix this, this and this," the naked back says, as if he is complimenting the woman when he points to her belly, breasts, and thighs. Can he possibly understand the loneliness of the stark reality the woman must return to after masturbating? Does he know that she can never feel sexual desire with her own body as it is, even in her imagination?

"It's tough for guys, too. Do you know how hard it is for us to get an erection? An erection, after all, maintains tension. And to maintain an erection, the man needs to feel more superior than the woman. He also needs to feel convinced that she desperately wants him to put his erection into her body."

The woman cannot understand an erection. Ob-

어쨌든 여자의 성기는 쾌락을 위해 존재하는 게 아니다. 배란과 수정이 이루어지는 생식 과정 자체가 그것을 증명하고 있다. 남자들은 오르가슴에 이르지 않으면, 정액이 분출되지 않는다. 하지만 여자들은 오르가슴과 상관없이, 한 달에 한 번 정기적으로 배란이 이루어진다. 여자가 쾌감을 느꼈나, 느끼지 못했나는 자연의 생식 과정에서 이미 제외되어버린 문제인 것이다.

"아까, 좋았어?"

잠에서 깨어난 벌거벗은 등이 돌아누우며 묻는다. 여자는 머쓱해하며 웃는다. 섹스를 하고 나면, 남자는 언제나 같은 질문을 하지만, 여자는 언제나 별로 할 말이 없다. 무엇이 좋았냐고 묻는 건지도 잘 알 수 없다.

"또 하고 싶어?"

어느 날 여자도 그에게 물었다. 그다지 예쁘지도 않고, 그다지 날씬하지도 않으며, 이따금 그가 알아듣지 못하는 엉뚱하고 이상한 이야기를 늘어놓는 자기를 왜 좋아하는지를. 그때 그는, 여자가 자기를 좋아해주기 때문에 여자가 좋다고 대답했다. 여자는 혼란을 느꼈다. 여자 또한 남자가 자기를 좋아해줘서 그를 좋아했기 때문이다. 그렇다면 남자와 여자가 서로 좋아한다는

viously there comes a moment when a woman is ready for sex, too—when she starts lubricating naturally. But a woman can have sex even when she is not ready, which is the greatest difference between a man and a woman. At the same time, this is also what a woman feels most pitiful about. When they are not in the mood for it or when they are not ready, there is no available apparatus in her body that allows her to refuse what she doesn't want.

Regardless, a female's genital organ does not exist for pleasure. The process of reproduction, from ovulation to fertilization, proves that. Men do not ejaculate if they do not reach orgasm, yet women regularly go through ovulation once a month—orgasm or no orgasm. Whether women feel pleasure or not is something already excluded from the process of reproduction.

"Did you enjoy it?" the naked back ask. He's awakened and he turns to her side. The woman smiles uncomfortably. After they have sex, the man always asks the same question, but the woman rarely has anything to say in response. She is not really sure what he is asking her she has enjoyed.

"Do you want to do it again?"

The woman realizes that his genital organ is still

관계로 엮인 지점은 도대체 어디서 시작된 것인가?

여자는 낯간지러운 가사로 가득 찬 유행가를 이메일로 보내던 남자를 기억한다. 언젠가는 전화를 걸어와 집 앞 골목길을 내다보라고 한 적도 있었다. 여자가 창문을 열고 골목을 향해 상체를 내밀자, 가로등 밑 어둠 속에서 남자는 유령처럼 스르륵 모습을 나타냈다. 그때 여자는 웃음이 날 것 같기도 하고 가슴이 뛰는 것 같기도 했다. 그렇게 진저리가 날 것처럼 달콤했던 남자의 모습을 여자는 가끔 떠올리곤 한다.

"이번에는 갈색 몸이야. 초콜릿 우유같이 매끄럽고 부드러운 몸이지. 길고 미끈한 갈색 다리가 거미처럼 내 허리를 휘감고 놔주지 않아."

나지막한 목소리로 중얼거리기 시작하던 남자의 목소리가 점점 묘한 열기를 뿜어내는 것을 여자는 느낀다. 동시에 여자의 손 안에서 남자의 성기가 조금씩 부풀어오르기 시작한다. 여자는 남자가 이미 아주 먼 곳으로 떠나버렸다는 것을 깨닫는다. 남자는 이제 촉촉하고 따뜻하게 벌어져 있는 갈색 몸의 붉은 입 속으로 자신을 밀어 넣으며, 한 손으로는 푸른 눈동자의 애벌레처럼 하얗게 부풀어오른 젖가슴을 움켜쥐고 있으리라.

in her hand.

One day the woman asked him why he liked her. After all, she was not very pretty or slim, and she often said strange things he did not understand. He responded by saying that he liked her because she liked him. The woman was confused by this answer; she liked him precisely because he liked her. How on earth, the woman asked herself, did their relationship start, with each one believing that the other liked them?

The woman remembers the same man who used to email her pop songs full of embarrassingly sweet lyrics. One day he called to tell her to look out at the lane in front of her house. When the woman opened the window and leaned out, the man gracefully appeared from under a streetlight like a phantom from the darkness. Her heart fluttered and she felt a mild desire to laugh. The woman recalls that sweet man, as sweet as to make her shudder at the thought.

"This time it's a brown body," the man says, thoughts of having sex with another woman dancing in his mind. "It's smooth and soft, like chocolate milk. When the woman spreads her legs, a pussy as black as a Hershey's chocolate bar in a nest of

여자가 아무리 남자를 좋아한다고 한들, 이제 남자의 욕망은 여자와는 상관없는 일이다. 남자는 자신의 욕망 속에서 홀로 외롭게 헤엄쳐 갈 것이다. 여자가 남자의 외로움을 위로하고 싶어 한들, 여자에게는 남자를 위로할 힘 같은 것은 없다. 어쩌면 외로운 것은 남자가 아니라 여자일지도 모른다. 아무래도 좋고, 어쨌든 크게 달라질 일은 없다고, 여자는 생각한다.

남자의 성기가 여자의 몸 안으로 들어온다. 오래된 상처의 딱지를 떼어내는 순간의 짜릿한 아픔 같기도 하고 쾌감 같기도 한 감각이 여자를 휘감는다. 여자는 눈을 감는다. 여자와 남자는 이제 한 몸이 되었으나, 서로 아주 먼 곳을 향해 멀어져가고 있다.

눈을 감은 여자의 머릿속에 하나의 그림이 떠오른다. 넘치는 햇살 아래 빛바랜 사진처럼 윤곽이 하얗게 흐려져 있던 억새밭. 오래전 여자는 외진 산길을 오르다 드넓은 억새밭과 마주친 적이 있었다. 키 큰 침엽수들로 빽빽이 들어 찬 어둑한 오솔길을 걷다가 갑작스레 눈앞이 환해져서 고개를 들어보니, 연한 자줏빛으로 넘실거리는 억새밭이 펼쳐져 있었다. 여자는 걸음을 멈췄다. 동행했던 사람들이 걱정이 되어 산길을 되짚어 내려올

golden hair appears... The long, sleek brown legs wrap themselves spider-like around my waist, and the legs don't let go."

The woman feels that the man's voice sounds increasingly full with a strange excitement. At the same time, the genital organ that was in her hand starts to swell little by little. She realizes that he has already gone to a place far away. Now, in his imagination, he is inserting himself into the red lips of the brown body, which are spread open, wet and warm. At the same time, he is grasping a blue-eyed woman's breast with one hand, her breast swollen white like a larva.

But however much she likes the man now, his desire does not have anything to do with her. He will swim alone in this desire. Even if she wants to console him in his loneliness, she has no power to do so. Or maybe it is the woman, not the man, who is lonely. She doesn't really care. Nothing will really change anyway, she thinks.

The man's genital organ enters her body. There is a sense of something embracing her, like the keen pain or pleasure of removing a scab from a scar formed long ago. The woman closes her eyes. She and the man have become one, even as they

때까지 여자는 억새밭을 떠날 수 없었다. 햇빛 속에서 은빛 솜털로 흔들리는 꽃송이들을 바라보면서, 여자는 나부끼는 억새꽃밭 속으로 옷을 다 벗고 천천히 걸어 들어가고 싶은 욕망을 느꼈다. 그저 단추를 풀고 소매를 걷어 올려, 드러난 팔뚝의 맨살로 억새꽃을 두어 번 쓰다듬었을 뿐이지만.

팔뚝에 돋은 소름이 여자의 온몸으로 퍼져나간다. 햇볕에 달아올라 이리저리 몸을 뒤척이는 억새밭 속으로 달려가는 꿈을, 여자는 꾸고 있다. 간지럽기도 하고 따갑기도 하고 아늑하기도 한 그 느낌 속으로 여자는 빠져 들어간다, 한없이. 여자는 귀를 기울인다. 으아 으아 으아악 억새꽃은 바람에 흐느끼고.

한때, 여자는, 손이 닿지 않는 먼 곳으로 떠나는 남자를 잡고 싶기도 했다.

……내가 잡을 수 있다고, 내가 너를 잡을 수 있다고, 내가 너의 것이고, 네가 나의 것이라고, 아늑하고 부드럽고 따뜻한 구멍 속으로 우리 둘이, 우리 둘만이 빠져 들어가, 나는 갈고리가 되어 너를 잡아당기고, 너는 내가 되고, 마침내 세상은 저 빛 속으로 사라지고, 우리는 하나의 꽃으로 활짝 피어날 것이라고…….

drift far away from each other.

An image appears in the woman's mind when she closes her eyes—a field of eulalia grass whose borders are blurred white like a faded photograph under the bright sunlight. Long ago, the woman came upon an enormous field of eulalia while climbing up a remote mountain path. She was walking along a dark section of the path that was crowded with tall coniferous trees when the field suddenly became bright before her eyes. As she lifted her head, the field of eulalia shone silver all over. The woman stopped walking. She could not leave the field until the people she was hiking with, who were probably worried about her by that point, reached her. The woman felt a desire to take off all her clothes and walk into the field of eulalia as she watched the silver tuft of grass tremble in the wind, flailing, rather, like it was struggling. Yet all she did was open the buttons on her sleeves, roll them, and caress the eulalia with the naked skin of her forearms a couple of times.

The goose bumps on her forearms spread all over her body. The woman dreams that she is running into the field of eulalia, which glow as they toss about under the sunlight. She becomes end-

어쩌면, 여자는, 아직 바라고 있는지도 모른다.

그러나 눈을 뜬 여자에게 보이는 것은, 빛바랜 벽지에 뭉개진 얼룩일 뿐인, 꽃이다.

『꽃』, 자음과모음, 2012

lessly absorbed in a feeling that is at once stinging and comfortable. She listens intently and hears something—the eulalia are sobbing in the wind.

There was once a time when the woman had wanted to grab on to the man as he left for that far-away place she could not reach.

I can grab on to you, I can do it. I am yours, and you are mine. We will enter that soft, warm opening, just the two of us; I'll become a hook and pull you, you become me. In the end, the world will disappear into the light, and we will bloom like a flower...

The woman still yearns for this.

Yet, when she opens her eyes, all she can see are flowers that are nothing but mere blotches, blotches mashed upon the faded wallpaper.

* English translation first published in the guarterly *ASIA*, No. 4.

Translated by Richard Harris and Kim Hyun-kyung

해설

Afterword

꽃을 해부하다

정은경 (문학평론가)

부희령의 「꽃」은 여성 성애에 대한 일종의 보고서이다. '보고서'라는 의미는 일체의 낭만적 시선이나 욕망의 투사를 배제하고 있다는 뜻이다. 부희령의 「꽃」은 한국문학에서 일찍이 보지 못했던 성에 대한 대담한 노출, 외설적인 장면들을 담고 있지만, 이 낯 뜨거운 문장들은 에로티시즘이나 성적 판타지와 전혀 무관하다. 오히려 그것은 일체의 낭만적 환상을 찢어내는, 냉정한 해부학자의 메스를 연상케 한다. 이 해부학자의 메스 앞에서 여성의 성기는 한낱 더럽고 퀴퀴한 냄새를 풍기는 '구멍'에 불과하다. 부희령은 이 '구멍'을 '꽃'이라는 수사와 대비시키면서 이 날것의 리얼리티를 극단적으로

Dissecting The Flower

Jung Eun-kyung (literary critic)

Pu Hee-ryoung's "Flowers" is a report of sorts on the female sexuality. It is a "report" because it is devoid of any romantic gaze or projections of desire. "Flowers" contains bold descriptions of sexuality and obscene scenes unprecedented in Korean literature, but these risqué sentences do not evoke eroticism or sexual fantasies in the least. Rather, it is reminiscent of a cold scalpel of an anatomist that cuts into and peels away all romantic fantasies. From this perspective, the genitals of a woman is nothing more than a dirty, musky-smelling "hole." By comparing this "hole" with the "flower," Pu takes the reality of this "raw thing" under a magnifying glass in the context of the social custom of patriar-

보여주는 동시에 여성의 성억압의 기원, 즉 한국사회의 뿌리 깊은 '남존여비'의 사회적 풍속을 함께 드러낸다.

이 소설은 화자이자 주인공인 '나'의 의문으로부터 출발한다. 드라마의 한 장면에서 한 여자가 "그래서 너는 그 애에게 네 꽃을 바쳤니?"라고 말하는 장면을 보고, '나'는 "여성의 성기를 왜 꽃에 비유하는 것일까?"라는 의문을 품는다. 성기와 섹슈얼리티의 생물학적 진상을 은폐하는 사회적 은유, 즉 '꽃'에 대한 해부는 이렇게 시작된다. 이 소설에서 주인공이 성에 눈뜨고 성에 탐닉하는 과정은 차라리 이 '꽃'이라는 화려한 수사를 배반하는 '아이러니'적 각성의 순간들이라고 할 수 있다.

주인공은 사춘기 시절 손거울로 자신의 성기를 들여다본다. 그녀는 자신의 성기가 꽃과는 아무런 상관이 없으며, 차라리 정육점의 고깃덩어리들과 흡사한 "기이한 열기와 뻔뻔스러운 광기까지 품고 있는" 육체의 일부에 불과하다는 것을 깨닫게 된다. 그녀는 이후 주위의 여자들을 보면서 그들의 치마 속에 존재하는 기괴한 구멍들을 떠올리곤 한다.

그리고 주인공은 서서히 성애에 눈뜨는 과정에서 자신의 성기를 애무하는 행위를 하다가 동생에게 발각된

chy—the origins of female sexual oppression—deeply embedded in Korean society.

This story begins with a question the protagonist poses. After watching a TV drama where one woman asks, "So did you offer him your flower?" she wonders why the female genital is compared to a flower. The dissection of the flower, a social metaphor that seeks to conceal the biological truth about genitals and sexuality, thus begins. The moments in the story when the protagonist discovers her sexuality and desires sex are ironic moments of revelation that undermines the charming "flower" metaphor.

As a teenager, the protagonist looks at her genitals with a hand mirror. She realizes that her genitals bear no resemblance to a flower and that it is nothing more than a part of her body that "even has a strange excitement to it, a shameless madness." They remind her of pieces of meat at the butcher shop. From then on, she looks at women around her at imagines the strange holes up their skirts.

The protagonist touches herself in the process of discovering her sexuality, and her younger sister catches her in the act. When the sister threatens to

다. 동생의 "엄마한테 이를 거야"라는 말을 듣고 '나'는 그러한 행동을 그만두게 되는데, 이 대목에는 어린 여성이 흔히 갖게 되는 '성의 억압과 죄의식과 자위에 대한 금기'가 고스란히 투영되어 있다. 주인공이 성에 눈뜸과 동시에 갖게 되는 죄의식은 "난 아빠가 술집 여자랑 뽀뽀하는 것 봤다"라고 말하는 동생의 귓속말과 함께 놓이면서 이를 더욱 증폭시킨다. 어린 여자의 성애는 아버지가 엄마 아닌 다른 여인과 통정하는 것과 등가관계에 놓인 엄청난 '비밀'이며 어둠의 진실인 것이다.

그 뒤 '나'는 사춘기를 거쳐 아이에서 여성으로 변모하는데, 이 변화 속에서 감정적, 육체적 혼란과 통증을 느낀다. '성장통'이라고 간단히 치부할 수 없는, 이 '죄의식과 두려움, 초조함'으로 범벅된 순간들을 작가 부희령은 섬세하고 핍진한 문체로 그려놓는다. 사춘기 무렵 어느 날 '나'는 아버지의 땀냄새에 이끌려 그 곁에 누웠다가 아버지로부터 "넌 여기서 뭐 하는 거야?"라는 짜증스러운 목소리와 함께 밀쳐지고 만다. '나'는 어지럼증을 느끼며 일어나 골목길로 나가 시멘트 담벼락에 손등을 긁으며 걸어간다.

tell on her, she gives it up. This scene is a reflection of the sexual oppression, guilt, andtaboo concerning masturbation.The guilt she feels as she discovers her sexuality isaugmented by her sister's whispered account, "I saw Dad kiss a bar maid." The sexuality of a young girl is a great, dark secret tantamount toa father's affair.

The protagonist transforms from a child to a woman through adolescence and experience emotional and physical confusion and pain in the process. Pu portrays these moments of "fear and anxiousness" with a delicate verisimilitude that cannot simply be labeled "growing pains." One day, the protagonist lies down next to her father, drawn by the smell of his sweat, and is pushed aside with an irritated, "What are you doing here?" Feeling dizzy, she gets up, and walks down the lane, "scratching the rough cement wall with a firmly clenched fist."

The back of her hand was grazed and felt sore. She continued walking along the empty lane. When she could not stand the pain any longer, she stopped and licked the back of her burning hand with her tongue. The smell of cement dust and blood entered her nostrils. With a sudden nausea, she threw up. While she was vomiting, leaning

"손등이 까져 쓰리고 아팠다. 여자애는 텅 빈 골목길을 자꾸자꾸 걸었다. 더 이상 아픔을 참을 수 없었을 때 여자애는 걸음을 멈추고 쓰린 손등을 혀로 핥았다. 시멘트 가루 냄새와 피비린내가 콧속을 파고들었고, 울컥 올라오는 구역질과 함께 여자애는 뱃속에 든 것을 게워냈다. 뜨거운 담벼락을 붙들고 토악질을 하는 여자애의 눈앞에 어둡고 텅 빈 구멍이 어른거렸다."

위의 인용문은 신체적으로 아이에서 여성으로 바뀌는 순간, 또는 정신분석학적으로 엘렉트라 콤플렉스를 넘는 순간에 대한 서정적 묘파라고 할 수 있다. 아버지, 혹은 페니스를 갈망하는 딸의 절망과 체념, 금기의 수용과 성적 성장을 작가는 저렇듯 예민하게 포착하여 시적으로 그려놓고 있는 것이다.

「꽃」은 이렇듯 '성기'를 둘러싼 몸의 생리를 냉정하게 그리고 있을 뿐 아니라, 사춘기 소녀의 감성과 성애와 관련한 심리를 해부하듯 치밀하게 파헤쳐놓고 있다. 가령, 강간당할 뻔했던 경험에 대해 "아주 짧은 순간이었지만, 소녀는 죽음의 공포를 느꼈다. 그리고 강간이 단지 억지로 성관계를 맺는 정도의 사건이 아니라는 사실

her hand against the hot summer day's wall, a dark, vacant hole wavered before the girl's eyes.

The scene quoted above is alyrical illustration of a moment when the a woman physically transforms from a child to a woman, or the psychoanalytical moment when she overcomes her Electra Complex. The despair and resignation of a daughter who desires the phallus represented by her father, the acceptance of taboo and the sexual growth is thus shrewdly captured and depicted poetically.

"Flowers" not simply an objective perspective on a biological process centered around the genitalia but also a detailed investigation on the psychology of an adolescent girl's sentiments and sexuality. For instance, a close encounter with rape is described as, "Although the encounter had been brief, the girl could feel the fear of death, and realized that rape was not just an incident where sex was had by force. Rape was something where, after someone was savagely beaten, a person or a person's character disappeared, and all that existed was a hole." And the first time she sees a penis she thinks, "the man's eyes were blurred with a strange excitement that glistened with great pride." And the sex scene

을 깨달았다. 강간은 무참하게 얻어맞은 끝에, 한 사람, 하나의 인격체는 사라지고, 그저 하나의 구멍만 존재하게 되는 일이었다" 혹은 주인공이 처음 남자의 성기를 보았을 때의 반응, "남자의 눈빛은 낯선 열기로 흐려져 있었으나, 한편으로 자랑스러움을 내보이며 반짝이고 있었기 때문이다" 등등. 그리고 이 성애학에 대한 보고서의 하이라이트이자 '성관계란 무엇인가'라는 근원적 질문을 불러오는 섹스의 장면에 이르기까지.

주인공은 첫 섹스에 대한 분홍빛 환상을 품고 남자친구와 섬에 간다. 그러나 섬의 한 가게 뒷방에서 치른 첫 관계에서 섹스에 관한 환상이 모조리 깨져버리고 만다. '사람들의 말소리와 술주정 소리가 끊임없이 들려오는' 뒷방에서 남자친구의 손길은 폭력처럼 변하고, '나'는 불안과 두려움으로 식은땀을 흘린다. 정사를 치른 뒤 남자가 남긴 "더러워"라는 말은 곧 이 환멸에 대한 정직한 고백인 셈이다. 그 뒤 주인공은 다른 남자들과의 섹스를 통해 라깡이 말한 '성관계의 불가능성'을 깨닫게 된다. 섹스가 끝난 뒤, 여자가 남자에게 묻는다. 왜 날 좋아하는지? 남자는 여자가 자기를 좋아해주기 때문이라고 말한다. 여자는 동일한 이유로 자신이 남자를 좋

that is the highlight of this report on sexuality and begs the fundamental question, "What is sex?"

The protagonist goes on a romantic trip to an island with a rosy fantasy of losing her virginity to her boyfriend. But all her fantasies are shattered as she has sex for the first time in the backroom of a store. The boyfriend's caresses turn violent in the backroom where she can hear the "drunken, frenzy-like yelling" of people outside, and cold sweat runs down the back of the anxious, frightened woman. "Dirty," says the man after the act, an honest confession on this disillusionment. After that, the protagonist comes to understand the "impossibility of sex" in the Lacanian sense. After having sex, the woman asks the man why he likes her. The man says it is because she likes him. The woman realizes that is the very reason she likes him as well. In other words, the affection they have for each other is, according to Lacan, a fantasy that disguisesthe sexual relationship that always falls short. Pu illustrates Lacan's observation that a "perfect union" is impossible by depicting a moment when the subject and the object disappears during the act of sex and all that remains is a hole.

아한다는 것을 깨닫는다. 즉 이들이 생각하는 상대방의 애정이란 라깡식으로 말하자면 언제나 어긋나는 성관계를 은폐하는 '환상'인 셈이다. 완전한 만남이란 불가능하다는 라깡의 고찰을 부희령은 섹스 과정에서 주체와 타자가 사라지고 '구멍'만 남은 순간으로 이렇게 재현하고 있다.

"남자의 성기가 여자의 몸 안으로 들어온다. 오래된 상처의 딱지를 떼어내는 순간의 짜릿한 아픔 같기도 하고 쾌감 같기도 한 감각이 여자를 휘감는다. 여자는 눈을 감는다. 여자와 남자는 이제 한 몸이 되었으나, 서로 아주 먼 곳을 향해 멀어져가고 있다."

부희령은 섹스의 거친 몸짓이 결국 멀리 달아나는 상대를 "내가 잡을 수 있다고, 내가 너를 잡을 수 있다고, (……) 아늑하고 부드럽고 따뜻한 구멍 속으로 우리 둘이, 우리 둘만이 빠져들어가, 나의 갈고리가 되어 너를 잡아당기고, 너는 내가 되고, 마침내 세상은 저 빛 속으로 사라지고, 우리는 하나의 꽃으로 활짝 피어날 것이라고" 믿고자 하는 처절한 몸부림임을 애도하고 있는

The man's genital organ enters her body. There is a sense of something embracing her, like the keen pain or pleasure derived in that moment she removes a scab from a scar formed long ago. The woman closes her eyes. She and the man have become one, even as they drift far away from each other.

Pu mourns the truth that the wild acts of sex is a desperate struggle to believe in the possibility with a lover who is drifting away: "I can grab on to you, I can do it, [...] we will enter the soft, warm hole, just the two of us; I will become a hook and pull you, you become me; in the end, the world will disappear into the light, and we will bloom like a flower..."

The sad clinical portrayal of sex we see in "Flowers" embodies a sociological meditation on Korean women, or perhaps women in general. The protagonist of the story is the fourth daughter of a family without sons and lives a life that began with her mother's weeping rather than blessings. The tradition of misogyny operates in her guilt, inferiority, and self-hatred. The fact that such social convention has caused women to envy the penis and drove their own sexuality into the dark does not elude Pu.

것이다.

「꽃」이 보여주는 섹스에 대한 슬픈 임상학에는 한국 여성, 혹은 여성에 대한 사회학적 고찰이 포함되어 있다. 이 작품에서 '나'는 딸만 내리 낳은 집의 '넷째 딸'로 태어나 축복이 아닌 '통곡'으로 시작된 삶을 산다. '나'의 죄의식, 열등감, 자기모멸에는 여성 비하의 전통이 작동하고 있는 것이다. 그러한 사회적 통념이 여성이 페니스를 선망하고 여성의 성을 어둠으로 스스로 몰아넣게 했다는 사실을 작가 부희령은 놓치지 않고 있는 것이다.

비평의 목소리

Critical Acclaim

부희령 소설들은 (……) 읽는 이로 하여금 일말의 판타지도 개재시킬 여지없는 지독한 세계를 보여준다. 때때로 그 세계는 출구가 없어 보여서 고통스럽기까지 하다. 물론 이 고통스러움은 좋은 소설, 나쁜 소설 등의 구분과는 관계가 없다. 만일 '쾌=즐거움=위안' 식의 일반적 통설에 기대거나 소설 바깥의 세속의 기준을 떠올린다면, 이것은 좋은 소설이 아닐지도 모른다. 사람들은 듣기 좋은 이야기, 자기 현재 상황을 잠시라도 눈감을 수 있는 이야기들을 좋은 것이라고 여기는 경향이 있기 때문이다. 그러나 그 듣기 좋고 읽기 좋은 이야기들이 끝나고 다시 현실로 돌아올 때 느낄 낙차는 또 다른 차

Pu Hee-ryoung's works [...] takes the reader to a nasty world that does not leave even the slightest room for fantastical relief. It's a painful world to be in, because there seems to be no way out. The pain caused by such stories is not a testament to the quality of the writing. Pu's stories do not fit the general expectations of "pleasure=joy=comfort" or any worldly criteria outside the scope of the story. People tend to believe that good stories are pleas-ant or allow even a moment's reprieve from their own harsh realities. But the "crash" of returning to reality once these happy stories are over is quite another matter because reality is in any case not

원의 문제이다. 현실은 어쨌든 소설이 아니기 때문이다. 이 소설집의 이야기들은 그런 의미의 낙차—간극의 문제로부터는 자유로울 것 같다. 이것은 체감하는 현실보다 더 불편한 현실의 이야기일 수 있고, 지금 여기의 발밑을 결코 떠나지 않기 때문이다. (……) 이것들은 모두, 우리네 생과 세계의 맨얼굴에 대한 충분한 르포로 읽히기도 한다. 그들의 불행과 고뇌를 들여다보고 있을 때 그 불가항력적 출구 없음에 대한 탄식을 피하기 어렵다. 삶의 맨얼굴을 이야기하는 소설들, 날것의 현실이 어떤 위장도 판타지도 없이 거울처럼 비춰지는 순간들은 때때로 당혹스럽다. 물론 이 이야기들은 결코 르포가 아니다. 그럼에도 르포에 가까운 리얼한 현실들이 조금의 타협도 없이 구체적으로 부감되는 것은, 근래 소설들을 떠올려볼 때 퍽 드문 것이기도 하다.

김미정

fiction. With the stories in this collection, readers will not have to worry about the harsh blow of returning to reality. The stories can be much more painful to swallow than reality itself, and the issues are so grounded in reality that it cannot be ignored. [...] These things can be read as a portrait our lives and world under all the heavy makeup. Peering into the misery and agony of the characters, it is difficult to not bemoan the inviolableexit-less-ness. The stories that deal with the naked faces of life and the moments when the rawness of reality is reflect without disguise or fantasy, like looking straight into a mirror, one is thrown off guard. Of course, these stories are definitely not reports of journalistic nature. However, it is a rare occurrence in fiction these days to find such detailed, uncompromising portraits of reality reminiscent of reports.

Kim Mi-jeong

부희령

서울에서 태어나 서울대학교에서 심리학을 공부했다. 어렸을 때부터 책읽기를 좋아해서 언젠가는 재밌는 책을 만드는 사람이 되겠다는 꿈을 가졌다. 책 만드는 사람은 되지 못했지만, 아이를 키우고, 살림을 하고, 농사를 짓고, 과외 선생 일을 하다가 마흔이 다 되어 뒤늦게 글 쓰는 일을 시작했다. 2001년《경향신문》신춘문예에「어떤 갠 날」이 당선되어 작품 활동을 시작했다. 지금은 소설 집필과 함께 번역가로도 활동하고 있다. 지은 책으로 소설집『꽃』과 청소년 소설『고양이 소녀』가 있고,『살아 있는 모든 것들』(Every living thing/Cynthia Rylant),『원챈스』(One chance : a memoir/Paul Potts)『에르미따』『샤나메』등 다수의 번역서가 있다.

Pu Hee-ryoung

Pu Hee-ryoung was born in Seoul and studied psychology at Seoul National University. An avid reader from a young age, her childhood dream was to make fun books. She never became an editor, but raised her children, managed her home, farmed, and tutored. At the age of forty, she started writing. She made her debut with "One Fine Day," which won *the Kyunghyang Shinmun* Spring Literary Contest in 2001. She is now a novelist and a translator. She has published a collection of short stories, *Flowers* and a young adult novel, *Cat Girl*, and has translated *Every Living Thing* by Cynthia Rylant and *One Chance: A Memoir* by Paul Potts, *Ermita, Shahnameh* among others.

번역 **리처드 해리스, 김현경**

Translated by Richard Harris and Kim Hyun-kyung

리처드 해리스는 두 권의 논픽션 도서 『한국의 로드맵』 『한국의 얼굴』과 소설집 『아버지의 아들』의 작가이다. 현재 캐나다 토론토에서 거주하고 있다. 그의 글쓰기에 관한 이야기는 홈페이지에 있다. http://harrisrichard.com/.

Richard Harris is the author of two non-fiction books, ***Roadmap to Korean*** and ***Faces of Korea***, and a novel, ***A Father's Son***. He lives in Toronto, Canada. Learn more about him and his writing at http://harrisrichard.com/.

김현경은 서강대학교 영어영문학과를 졸업하고 외국계 사무소와 출판사에서 근무했다. 다양한 번역서와 비평지를 편집했고, 현재 편집과 번역을 하고 있다.

Kim Hyun-kyung is an editor and translator. She studied English Literature at Sogang University before beginning work at Korea Office at Wisconsin's Department of Development. Later she served as an editor at several Korean publishing companies. She has edited many books that have been translated from English into Korean as well as working at The Journal of Design Culture and Criticism.

감수 **전승희, 데이비드 윌리엄 홍**

Edited by Jeon Seung-hee and David William Hong

전승희는 서울대학교와 하버드대학교에서 영문학과 비교문학으로 박사 학위를 받았으며, 현재 하버드대학교 한국학 연구소의 연구원으로 재직하며 아시아 문예 계간지 《ASIA》 편집위원으로 활동 중이다. 현대 한국문학 및 세계문학을 다룬 논문을 다수 발표했으며, 바흐친의 『장편소설과 민중언어』, 제인 오스틴의 『오만과 편견』 등을 공역했다. 1988년 한국여성연구소의 창립과 《여성과 사회》의 창간에 참여했고, 2002년부터 보스턴 지역 피학대 여성을 위한 단체인 '트랜지션하우스' 운영에 참여해 왔다. 2006년 하버드대학교 한국학 연구소에서 '한국 현대사와 기억'을 주제로 한 워크숍을 주관했다.

Jeon Seung-hee is a member of the Editorial Board of ***ASIA***, and a Fellow at the Korea Institute, Harvard University. She received a Ph.D. in English Literature from Seoul National University and a Ph.D. in Comparative Literature from Harvard University. She has presented and published numerous papers on modern Korean and world literature. She is also a co-translator of Mikhail Bakhtin's ***Novel and***

the People's Culture and Jane Austen's ***Pride and Prejudice***. She is a founding member of the Korean Women's Studies Institute and of the biannual Women's Studies' journal ***Women and Society*** (1988), and she has been working at 'Transition House,' the first and oldest shelter for battered women in New England. She organized a workshop entitled "The Politics of Memory in Modern Korea" at the Korea Institute, Harvard University, in 2006. She also served as an advising committee member for the Asia-Africa Literature Festival in 2007 and for the POSCO Asian Literature Forum in 2008.

데이비드 윌리엄 홍은 미국 일리노이주 시카고에서 태어났다. 일리노이대학교에서 영문학을, 뉴욕대학교에서 영어교육을 공부했다. 지난 2년간 서울에 거주하면서 처음으로 한국인과 아시아계 미국인 문학에 깊이 몰두할 기회를 가졌다. 현재 뉴욕에서 거주하며 강의와 저술 활동을 한다.

David William Hong was born in 1986 in Chicago, Illinois. He studied English Literature at the University of Illinois and English Education at New York University. For the past two years, he lived in Seoul, South Korea, where he was able to immerse himself in Korean and Asian-American literature for the first time. Currently, he lives in New York City, teaching and writing.

바이링궐 에디션 한국 대표 소설 069
꽃

2014년 6월 6일 초판 1쇄 인쇄 | 2014년 6월 13일 초판 1쇄 발행

지은이 부희령 | **옮긴이** 리처드 해리스, 김현경 | **펴낸이** 김재범
감수 전승희, 데이비드 윌리엄 홍 | **기획** 정은경, 전성태, 이경재
편집 정수인, 이은혜 | **관리** 박신영 | **디자인** 이춘희
펴낸곳 (주)아시아 | **출판등록** 2006년 1월 27일 제406-2006-000004호
주소 서울특별시 동작구 서달로 161-1(흑석동 100-16)
전화 02.821.5055 | **팩스** 02.821.5057 | **홈페이지** www.bookasia.org
ISBN 979-11-5662-018-1 (set) | 979-11-5662-031-0 (04810)
값은 뒤표지에 있습니다.

Bi-lingual Edition Modern Korean Literature 069
Flowers

Written by Pu Hee-ryoung | **Translated by** Richard Harris and Kim Hyun-kyung
Published by Asia Publishers | 161-1, Seodal-ro, Dongjak-gu, Seoul, Korea
Homepage Address www.bookasia.org | **Tel**. (822).821.5055 | **Fax**. (822).821.5057
First published in Korea by Asia Publishers 2014
ISBN 979-11-5662-018-1 (set) | 979-11-5662-031-0 (04810)

〈바이링궐 에디션 한국 대표 소설〉 작품 목록(1~60)

아시아는 지난 반세기 동안 한국에서 나온 가장 중요하고 첨예한 문제의식을 가진 작가들의 작품들을 선별하여 총 105권의 시리즈를 기획하였다. 하버드 한국학 연구원 및 세계 각국의 우수한 번역진들이 참여하여 외국인들이 읽어도 어색함이 느껴지지 않는 손색없는 번역으로 인정받았다. 이 시리즈는 세계인들에게 문학 한류의 지속적인 힘과 가능성을 입증하는 전집이 될 것이다.

바이링궐 에디션 한국 대표 소설 set 1

분단 Division

01 병신과 머저리-**이청준** The Wounded-**Yi Cheong-jun**
02 어둠의 혼-**김원일** Soul of Darkness-**Kim Won-il**
03 순이삼촌-**현기영** Sun-i Samch'on-**Hyun Ki-young**
04 엄마의 말뚝 1-**박완서** Mother's Stake I-**Park Wan-suh**
05 유형의 땅-**조정래** The Land of the Banished-**Jo Jung-rae**

산업화 Industrialization

06 무진기행-**김승옥** Record of a Journey to Mujin-**Kim Seung-ok**
07 삼포 가는 길-**황석영** The Road to Sampo-**Hwang Sok-yong**
08 아홉 켤레의 구두로 남은 사내-**윤흥길** The Man Who Was Left as Nine Pairs of Shoes-**Yun Heung-gil**
09 돌아온 우리의 친구-**신상웅** Our Friend's Homecoming-**Shin Sang-ung**
10 원미동 시인-**양귀자** The Poet of Wŏnmi-dong-**Yang Kwi-ja**

여성 Women

11 중국인 거리-**오정희** Chinatown-**Oh Jung-hee**
12 풍금이 있던 자리-**신경숙** The Place Where the Harmonium Was-**Shin Kyung-sook**
13 하나코는 없다-**최윤** The Last of Hanak'o-**Ch'oe Yun**
14 인간에 대한 예의-**공지영** Human Decency-**Gong Ji-young**
15 빈처-**은희경** Poor Man's Wife-**Eun Hee-kyung**

바이링궐 에디션 한국 대표 소설 set 2

자유 Liberty

16 필론의 돼지-**이문열** Pilon's Pig-**Yi Mun-yol**
17 슬로우 불릿-**이대환** Slow Bullet-**Lee Dae-hwan**
18 직선과 독가스-**임철우** Straight Lines and Poison Gas-**Lim Chul-woo**
19 깃발-**홍희담** The Flag-**Hong Hee-dam**
20 새벽 출정-**방현석** Off to Battle at Dawn-**Bang Hyeon-seok**

사랑과 연애 Love and Love Affairs

21 별을 사랑하는 마음으로-**윤후명** With the Love for the Stars-**Yun Hu-myong**
22 목련공원-**이승우** Magnolia Park-**Lee Seung-u**
23 칼에 찔린 자국-**김인숙** Stab-**Kim In-suk**
24 회복하는 인간-**한강** Convalescence-**Han Kang**
25 트렁크-**정이현** In the Trunk-**Jeong Yi-hyun**

남과 북 South and North

26 판문점-**이호철** Panmunjom-**Yi Ho-chol**
27 수난 이대-**하근찬** The Suffering of Two Generations-**Ha Geun-chan**
28 분지-**남정현** Land of Excrement-**Nam Jung-hyun**
29 봄 실상사-**정도상** Spring at Silsangsa Temple-**Jeong Do-sang**
30 은행나무 사랑-**김하기** Gingko Love-**Kim Ha-kee**

바이링궐 에디션 한국 대표 소설 set 3

서울 Seoul

31 눈사람 속의 검은 항아리-**김소진** The Dark Jar within the Snowman-**Kim So-jin**
32 오후, 가로지르다-**하성란** Traversing Afternoon-**Ha Seong-nan**
33 나는 봉천동에 산다-**조경란** I Live in Bongcheon-dong-**Jo Kyung-ran**
34 그렇습니까? 기린입니다-**박민규** Is That So? I'm A Giraffe-**Park Min-gyu**
35 성탄특선-**김애란** Christmas Specials-**Kim Ae-ran**

전통 Tradition

36 무자년의 가을 사흘-**서정인** Three Days of Autumn, 1948-**Su Jung-in**
37 유자소전-**이문구** A Brief Biography of Yuja-**Yi Mun-gu**
38 향기로운 우물 이야기-**박범신** The Fragrant Well-**Park Bum-shin**
39 월행-**송기원** A Journey under the Moonlight-**Song Ki-won**
40 협죽도 그늘 아래-**성석제** In the Shade of the Oleander-**Song Sok-ze**

아방가르드 Avant-garde

41 아겔다마-**박상륭** Akeldama-**Park Sang-ryoong**
42 내 영혼의 우물-**최인석** A Well in My Soul-**Choi In-seok**
43 당신에 대해서-**이인성** On You-**Yi In-seong**
44 회색 時-**배수아** Time In Gray-**Bae Su-ah**
45 브라운 부인-**정영문** Mrs. Brown-**Jung Young-moon**

바이링궐 에디션 한국 대표 소설 set 4

디아스포라 Diaspora

46 속옷-**김남일** Underwear-**Kim Nam-il**
47 상하이에 두고 온 사람들-**공선옥** People I Left in Shanghai-**Gong Sun-ok**
48 모두에게 복된 새해-**김연수** Happy New Year to Everyone-**Kim Yeon-su**
49 코끼리-**김재영** The Elephant-**Kim Jae-young**
50 먼지별-**이경** Dust Star-**Lee Kyung**

가족 Family

51 혜자의 눈꽃-**천승세** Hye-ja's Snow-Flowers-**Chun Seung-sei**
52 아베의 가족-**전상국** Ahbe's Family-**Jeon Sang-guk**
53 문 앞에서-**이동하** Outside the Door-**Lee Dong-ha**
54 그리고, 축제-**이혜경** And Then the Festival-**Lee Hye-kyung**
55 봄밤-**권여선** Spring Night-**Kwon Yeo-sun**

유머 Humor

56 오늘의 운세-**한창훈** Today's Fortune-**Han Chang-hoon**
57 새-**전성태** Bird-**Jeon Sung-tae**
58 밀수록 다시 가까워지는-**이기호** So Far, and Yet So Near-**Lee Ki-ho**
59 유리방패-**김중혁** The Glass Shield-**Kim Jung-hyuk**
60 전당포를 찾아서-**김종광** The Pawnshop Chase-**Kim Chong-kwang**